The Duckling Gets a Cookie!?

to Cher,
one sweet cookie

I do not like
the look of
that title.

ISBN 978-C-545-81671-7

Text and illustrations copyright © 2012 by Mo Willems.
All rights reserved. Published by Scholastic Inc.,
557 Broadway, New York, NY 10012,
by arrangement with Hyperion Books for Children,
an imprint of Disney Book Group.
SCHOLASTIC and associated logos are
trademarks and/or registered trademarks of Scholastic Inc.

12 11 10 9 8 7 6 5 4 3 2   15 16 17 18 19/0

Printed in the U.S.A.   08

First Scholastic printing, October 2014

The Duckling Gets a Cookie!?

words and pictures by mo willems

SCHOLASTIC INC.

Oh!

I'll ask for a "French Fry Robot" every now and then.

I've asked for a walrus!

Right now, I'm asking, "Why?"

Why? WHY? WHY?

Ohhhh... there's more!

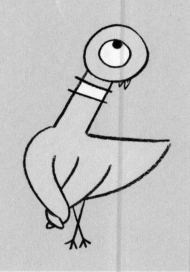

Sometimes I ask for a hug.

Or I'll ask for one more story!

I can't count the times I've asked for my own personal iceberg.

WHY DID YOU GET THAT COOKIE!?!

So I could give it to you.

Bye!

May I have
another cookie,
please?

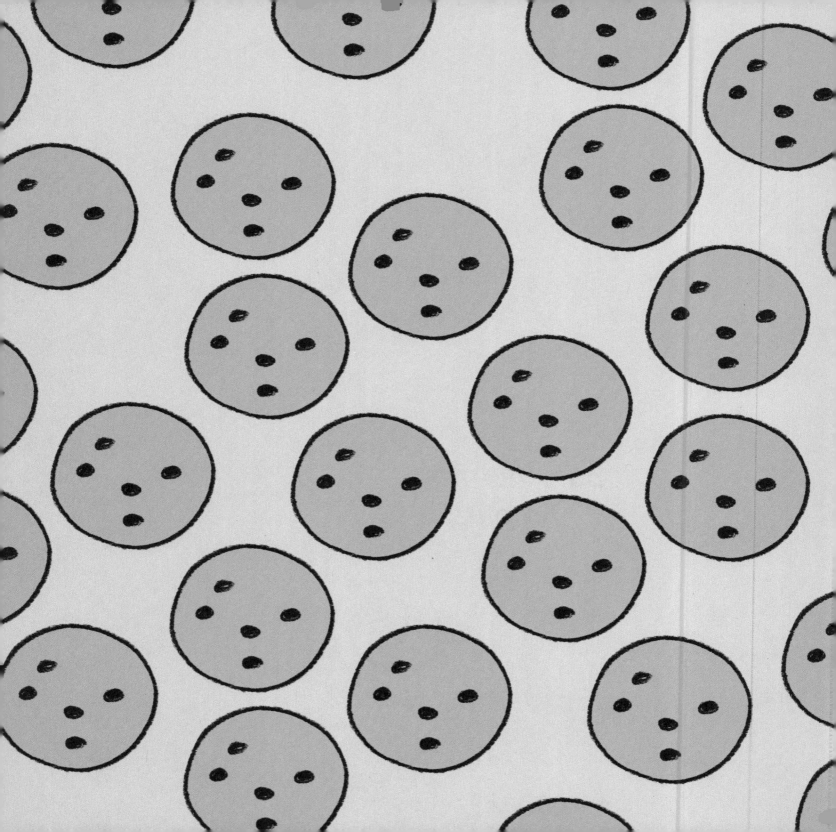

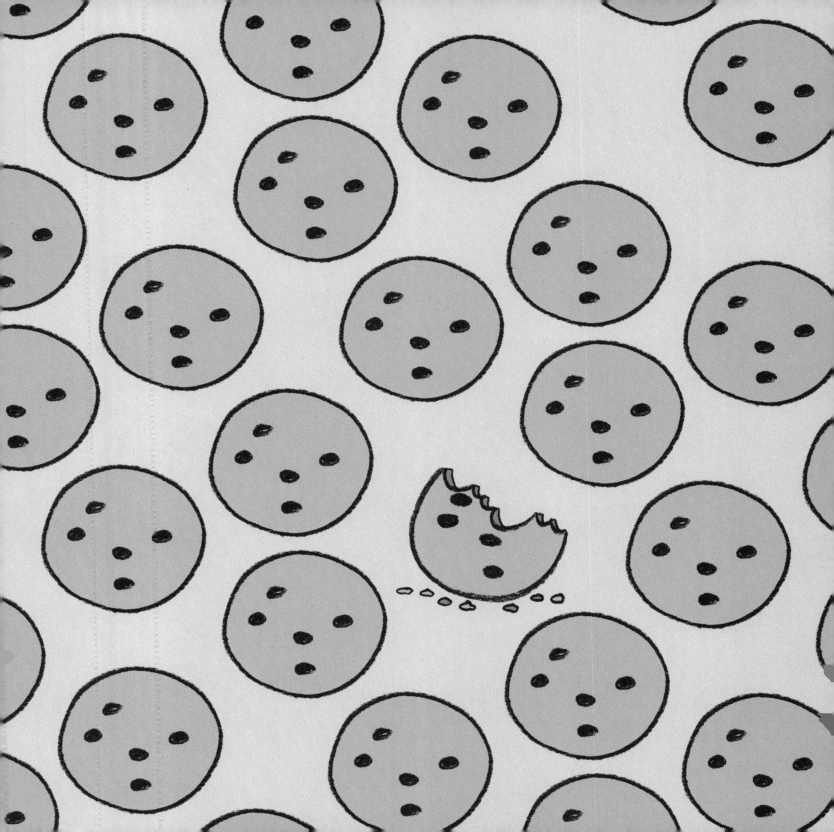